A Windy Day

Written by Margo Gates

Illustrated by Sarah Jennings

GRL Consultants, Diane Craig and Monica Marx,
Certified Literacy Specialists

Lerner Publications ◆ Minneapolis

Note from a GRL Consultant
This Pull Ahead leveled book has been carefully designed for beginning readers. A team of guided reading literacy experts has reviewed and leveled the book to ensure readers pull ahead and experience success.

Lerner Publications Company
A division of Lerner Publishing Group, Inc.
241 First Avenue North
Minneapolis, MN 55401 USA

For reading levels and more information, look up this title at www.lernerbooks.com.

Main body text set in Mikado 24/41
Typeface provided by Hannes von Doehren.

The images in this book are used with the permission of: Sarah Jennings

Library of Congress Cataloging-in-Publication Data

Names: Gates, Margo, author. | Jennings, Sarah, illustrator.
Title: A windy day / by Margo Gates ; illustrated by Sarah Jennings.
Description: Minneapolis : Lerner Publications, [2020] | Series: Let's look at weather (Pull ahead readers - Fiction) | Includes index.
Identifiers: LCCN 2018057294 (print) | LCCN 2018057816 (ebook) | ISBN 9781541562172 (eb pdf) | ISBN 9781541558434 (lb : alk. paper) | ISBN 9781541573208 (pb : alk. paper)
Subjects: LCSH I: Readers (Primary) | Winds—Juvenile fiction.
Classification: LCC PE1119 (ebook) | LCC PE1119 .G38485 2020 (print) | DDC 428.6/2—dc23

LC record available at https://lccn.loc.gov/2018057294

Manufactured in the United States of America
3-50505-46224-4/1/2021

Contents

A Windy Day

Jay and Tara went out to play.

"Today is a windy day," said Tara.

"Where do you see the wind today?" asked Jay.

"I see it in the trees," Tara said. "The trees bend in the wind."

"I see it in the leaves," said Tara.
"The leaves blow in the wind."

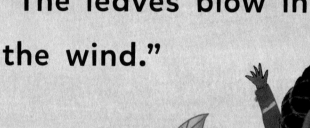

The wind blew and blew.
"My hat is blowing away,"
said Tara.

"I see the wind," said Jay.
"Your hair is blowing in
the wind."

Did You See It?

hair

leaves

out

trees

wind

Index